P9-DTG-046

This
book
belongs
to

_____

Young Readers Book Club presents...

I MEANT TO CLEAN MY ROOM TODAY

I MEANT TO CLEAN MY ROOM TODAY

written and illustrated by

Miriam Nerlove

Margaret K. McElderry Books

NEW YORK

Copyright © 1988 by Miriam Nerlove
All rights reserved. No part of this book may be reproduced or transmitted
in any form or by any means, electronic or mechanical, including photocopying,
recording, or by any information storage and retrieval system,
without permission in writing from the Publisher.

Margaret K. McElderry Books
Macmillan Publishing Company
866 Third Avenue
New York, NY 10022
Collier Macmillan Canada, Inc.

Text composition by Linoprint Composition, New York, New York

A B C D   0 1 2 3

Library of Congress Cataloging-in-Publication Data

Nerlove, Miriam.
I meant to clean my room today.

Summary: A child describes all the things that
prevented her from cleaning her room.
[1. Cleanliness—Fiction.   2. Orderliness—
Fiction.   3. Stories in rhyme]   I. Title.
PZ8.3.N365Im   1988   [E]   87-16968
ISBN 0-689-50438-1

The original pictures for *I Meant to Clean My Room Today*
are watercolor paintings.

Grolier Enterprises Inc. offers a varied selection of
children's book racks and tote bags. For details on
ordering, please write: Grolier Enterprises Inc.,
Sherman Turnpike, Danbury, CT 06816 Attn:
Premium Department

For Howard, with love,
and special thanks to Margaret

I meant to clean my room today—

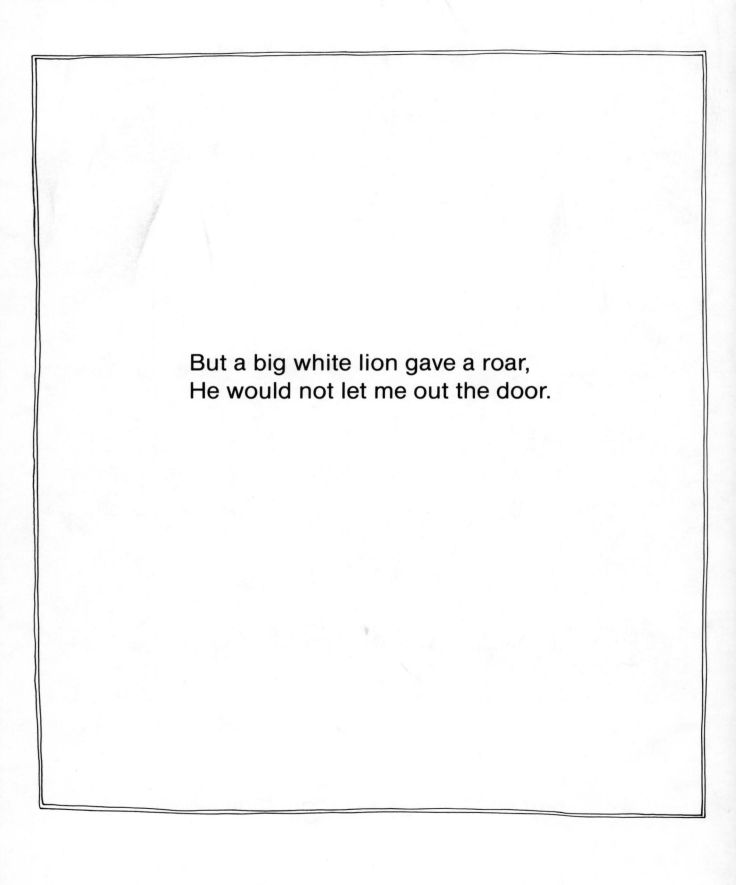

But a big white lion gave a roar,
He would not let me out the door.

A yellow turtle crawled to my bed,
He showed me how to stand on my head.

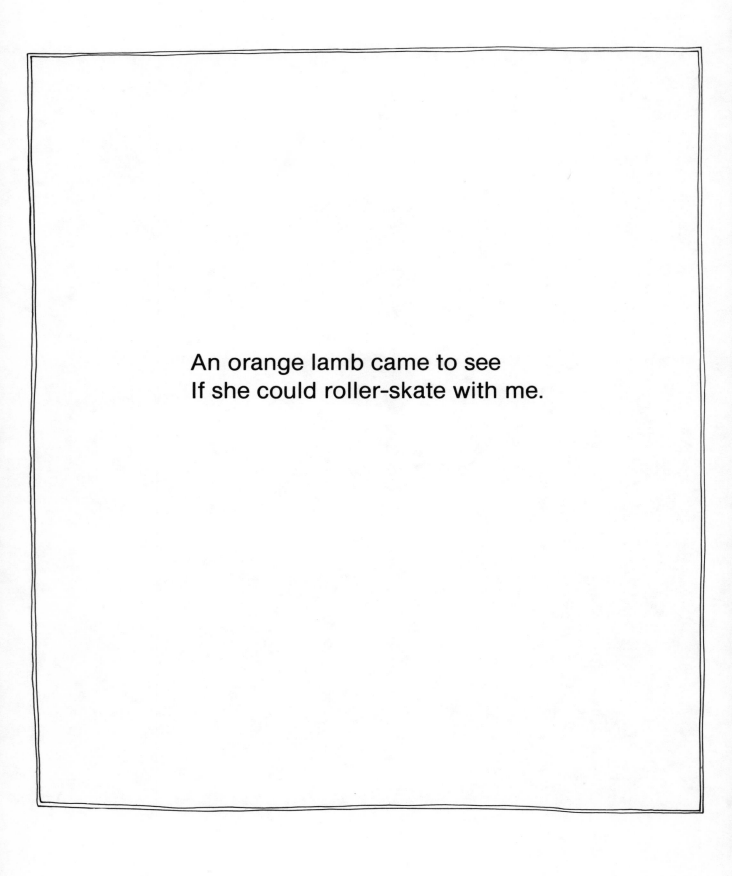

An orange lamb came to see
If she could roller-skate with me.

And a green kitten romped on the floor,
She chewed my clothes and got stuck in a drawer.

A fat blue pig came to get clean,
I filled up the tub—so as not to be mean.

A red giraffe arrived at noon,
He asked me if I'd sing a tune.

And a big beige bunny hopped in for lunch,
We had chocolate ice cream and strawberry punch.

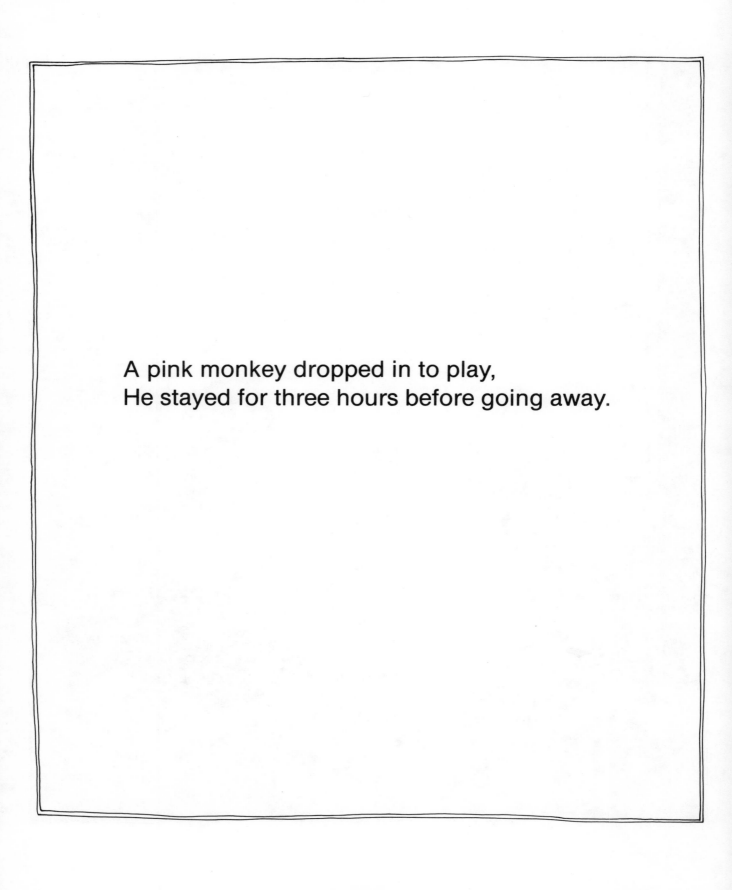

A pink monkey dropped in to play,
He stayed for three hours before going away.

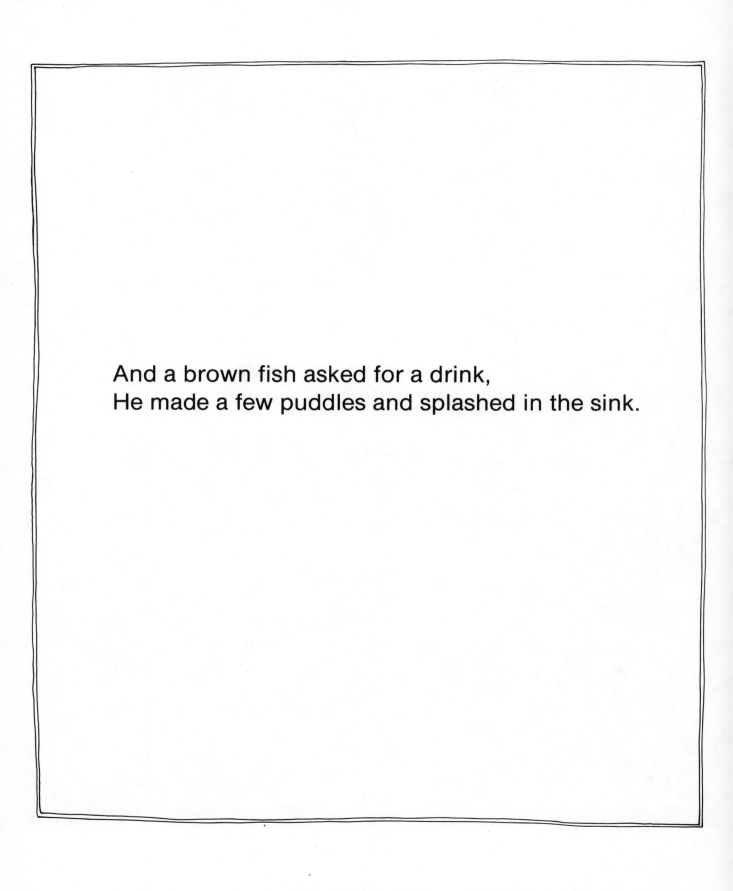

And a brown fish asked for a drink,
He made a few puddles and splashed in the sink.

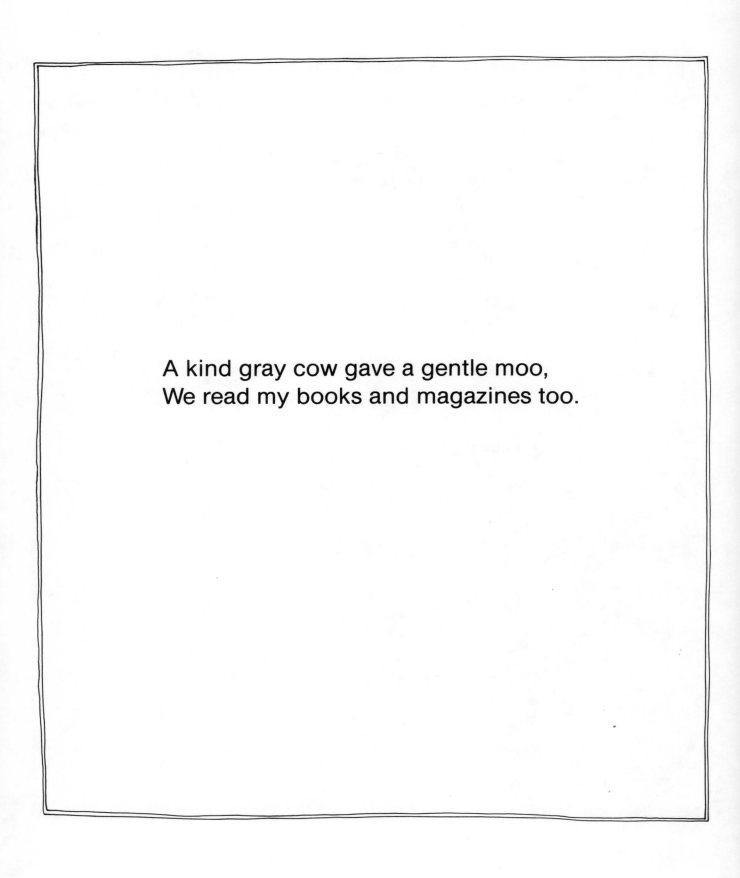

A kind gray cow gave a gentle moo,
We read my books and magazines too.

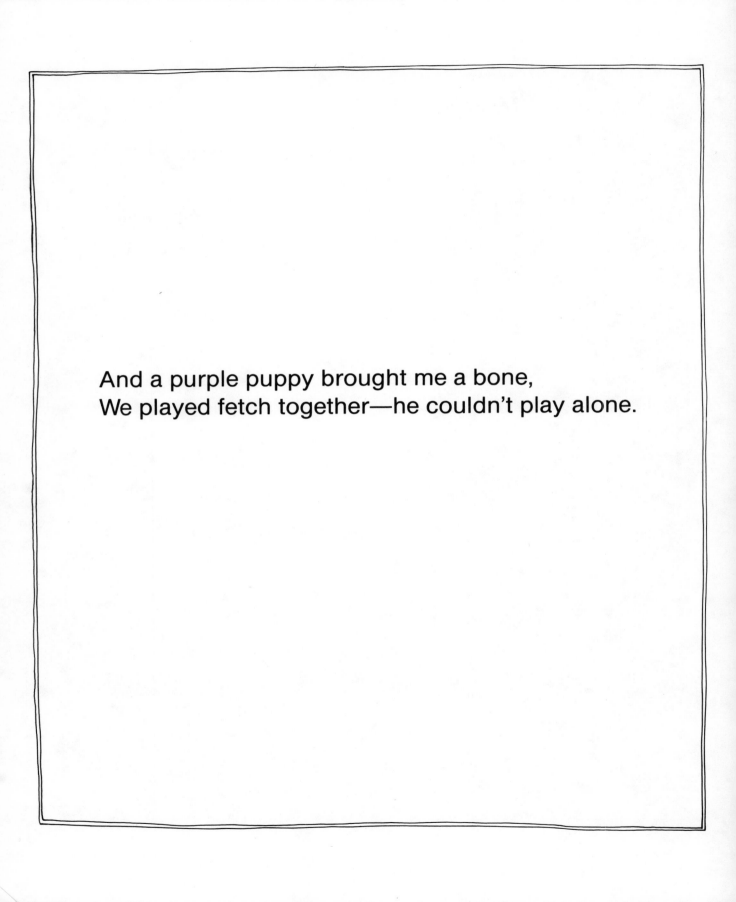

And a purple puppy brought me a bone,
We played fetch together—he couldn't play alone.

A rainbow parrot brought me some flowers,
We sat down to visit and gossiped for hours.

I meant to clean my room today,
But other things got in the way.